"When you're sitting on top of the world, every way you point is down.
. . . on a map, down is always South . . ."

The Star on the Pole

A story told by
Captain Horatio Oldsalt
to R.W. (Bob) Thompson, Jr.,
illustrated by
Roderick K. Keitz,
and published by
The North Pole Chronicles

It was morning when Captain Horatio Oldsalt headed toward his workshop to show the elves how to make a new bathtub toy for Christmas.

A fresh snow had fallen during the night
and the captain's peg leg made it hard to walk without slipping.
"I wish I had worn snowshoes or at least brought a cane," he mumbled.
"There sure won't be any dashing through the snow today!"

When he passed the North Pole, he saw that
three of the four pointers that say SOUTH were missing.
"That's strange. I wonder what happened to them?" he thought.
Then he noticed a path of footprints leading to the pole
and some more footprints going away from it.

"Those must be Pout's prints," Oldsalt exclaimed when he looked at them.
It was easy to tell that they were Pout's
since he was the only elf who was born with two left feet.

Captain Oldsalt followed the trail of footprints
to the workshop where Michael and Jello paint signs for Santa.

"Why have you brought those SOUTH pointers here?" Oldsalt asked.
"I am going to have Michael and Jello repaint them
so one will say NORTH, one EAST, and one WEST," Pout proudly replied.
"Then all of the North Pole's pointers won't just say SOUTH."

"You'd better not, Pout, I'm telling you why," said the wise old sea captain.
"The world is like a ball with the North Pole right on top of it.
When you're sitting on top of the world, every way you point is down.
Since on a map down is always South,
every pointer on the North Pole **must** say South.

Now, let's take these SOUTH signs and put them back on the pole."

As they walked back to the North Pole, Pout and Oldsalt enjoyed the smell of
a fresh batch of candy canes that the Mushroom Heads were cooking.
The smell was so tempting that they stopped by Suzie Scheff's workshop
to get a few canes for themselves.

When they got to the pole and were putting the pointers back on it,
Pout asked Oldsalt why the pole had red stripes painted around it.
"Because Santa likes candy canes, too," Oldsalt replied with a smile.
"He thought it would be fun to paint the North Pole to look like
a great big stick of peppermint candy. And it does!"

"Is the star on top of the pole just for fun, too?" asked Pout.
"No, no, a thousand times no," said a suddenly serious Oldsalt.
"When it's dark, if you stand next to the pole and look up,
you'll see a very bright star. It's called the North Star,
and the North Star is very important to Santa."

"On Christmas Eve,
when he finishes delivering toys to all of the good girls and boys,
Santa turns his sleigh and points it at the North Star.
He knows that if he flies straight toward it,
he'll end up right over the North Pole.
Then all he has to do is land his sleigh and he'll be home."

"Finding the North Star is easy for Santa," continued the captain,
"He takes his sleigh high above the clouds
and then looks for a group of bright stars that together form a constellation
that looks like a great big pail that is used for dipping water.
This constellation is called the Big Dipper."

"At the end opposite from the handle of the Big Dipper
are two stars that make the end of the pail.
They point directly toward that very bright star, the North Star.
If you look a little longer, you will see that the North Star is at the end of the
handle of a smaller pail that is formed by another group of stars.
Since this pail is smaller, it's known as the Little Dipper."

"Being able to rely on the North Star means a lot to Santa.
He knows it will always be there to help him find his way home
after his long Christmas Eve trip.
That's why he put a star on the top of the North Pole.

It's his way of saying, 'Thank you, old reliable friend.
I can always count on you.'"

Pout was tired of the pole and pail talk.
He wanted some more candy.
He convinced Captain Oldsalt to go back to Suzie Scheff's shop
where they could both get another candy cane.

Suzie happened to look out her window
just as the pair was coming down Santa Claus Lane.
She noticed that Oldsalt was having a hard time walking in the snow.

As soon as they got into the workshop,
one of the Mushroom heads gave Pout a candy cane.
Giving an extra large one to Oldsalt, Suzie said,
"Try using this. It might make walking in the snow easier for you."
"Thank you, I will," Oldsalt said, and then he muttered to himself,
"Imagine that, a candy-cane cane."

Turning to Pout, Captain Oldsalt said, "Now, little buddy,
I must be going to my workshop to show the elves a new toy.
It's been fun being with you this morning."

As Oldsalt walked across the snow, Pout chuckled at the sight of
the old sea captain with his candy-cane cane
and the funny looking footprints they made in the snow.